Prince of Flies

An Esar-Haden Tale

H. Rad Bethlen

Rooster & Raven

Library of Congress Control Number: 2024948720

For the Daughters of Zeus and Mnemosyne

Author Statement Concerning Artificial Intelligence

The way I write consist of several phases.

1. Idea generation.
2. Research.
3. Story development.
4. Outlining.
5. Writing the rough draft.
6. Editing and rewriting.
7. Editing and polishing.
8. Copy editing.

I will *occasionally* use AI during the research phase if I can't locate some bit of information on my own—but I try to locate it on my own first.

I will *occasionally* use AI during the story's development if I get stuck on something—but I try to resolve my own story issues first.

I *intentionally* use AI during the copy editing phase as a stand-in for a copy editor, which I can't afford to pay for yet which I don't want to go without.

A copy editor is the last set of eyes to look at a manuscript to check for grammar, usage, spelling, and punctuation mistakes. I ask the AI copy editor to make suggestions on corrections. I evaluate those suggestions. If I agree, I make the changes.

I don't use AI for anything else.

Be comforted that this story was written by a human being for other human beings.

H. Rad Bethlen

Prince Lewin lay on his side, pained from a fall from the saddle. What had knocked him down he did not know.

Wind howled through the stones and lashed his body, causing him to curl himself in defense against its bite. He was not dressed for cold and even though he wore armor it held in none of his body's warmth. He felt what he thought was sand strike his face, for he had been in the desert. However, the wind was bitterly cold and the "sand" was wet on his flesh. The wind turned. He tried to open his eyes but could not. He reached up and scraped the ice free from his face. He opened his eyes only to close them as the wind shifted back. It stayed but a moment before again changing direction. He sat up, shielded himself with an upraised hand, and looked.

Before him was the entrance to Pwyll, but not as he had last seen it. The defensive earthworks built by the dark elves were hidden by a frozen cascade of water, the origin of which he could not divine. He looked around. The hard-packed desert floor was covered with shimmering ice. Tendrils of snow shot in whichever direction the capricious wind desired.

Near him, the iron-shod hooves and long, bony-kneed legs of a horse rose, hooves high, from the ice. He was surrounded by horses, locked in various poses by ice and death. His own horse was close. He saw its head in profile: black lips curled, tongue hanging over blocky yellow teeth, flared nostrils frosted, mane glued by frozen blood, and a thin ledge of snow building on the curved surface of its glossy black eyes.

Prince Lewin struggled to his feet. He checked himself for injury and while sore he saw no wounds, felt no broken bones. He held his palm against the wind and looked around. Littered amongst the horses were dead dark elves. They, too, had been claimed by the ice. Their black armor resembled the backs of beetles caught in a sudden snow. Their white hair was lost in that other white. He saw wagons and siege works blackened by fire. The wind pulled ash from these carcasses, mingled it with the snow, and hid the sun with its swirling.

Opposite the ice-choked entrance, at the edge of the field of battle, Prince Lewin saw a dark elf female sitting cross-legged on the ice. She wore thick furs but her head, forearms, and hands were exposed. Her long white hair danced like a flag of surrender. He squinted and studied her. A half-mask hid the upper part of her face and made it alien. He could see puffs of breath escape from her moving lips.

He pulled his sword free and approached. The dark elf woman was chanting in prayer. Now closer, he could make out the mask. It was black with a sparse coating of short, stiff, black hairs. The eyes were bulbous, shimmering, and multifaceted. The brilliance of the frozen scene was multiplied on the hundredfold surface of those eyes. The mask depicted a fly's face. He saw movement and looked to her forearms and hands. They were coated with congealed blood. Flies clung to her, their translucent wings bending in the wind. The swarm fed on the blood, sponging it, mopping it up with a thousand eager mouths.

'How do they survive the cold?'

The wind blew. The flies were not swept away.

'Or maintain their grip?'

Prince Lewin was about to speak when the wind pooled into a vortex about him, throwing up snow and ash, forcing him to close his eyes. The vortex was short-lived. When he opened his eyes the dark elf was gone. He saw movement where she had been. He thought it might be the flies, approached, knelt and examined them. It was not the flies, however, nor was the movement on the ice, but under it. He bent closer and saw with horror that there was a soldier under the ice who wore the colors of the Crown.

The soldier floated in a void. Only his face, shoulders, and uplifted arms could be seen. The rest of him was sunk in darkness. He had a wound on his forehead. Blood ran over the bridge of his nose, caught the slope of his cheek, fell, and vanished into the darkness. The soldier saw the prince and began to beat against the underside of the ice with his bloodied fists. He screamed for the prince's aid, his mouth twisting, but no sound reached Lewin's ears.

Prince Lewin dropped fully to his knees and beat the pommel of his sword against the ice. Flecks of ice launched into the air. The man trapped beneath the ice looked to his side. When he looked back his eyes were wide with fear. This contagious emotion spread to the prince, who slammed his pommel with all of his strength. With an ear-piercing crack the blade of his sword shattered into glittering shards. The handle split in his hand. The pommel shot off and disappeared in the snow.

He flinched away from the shattering of the blade. The metal bounced against the armor of his shoulder and arm and came to rest on the ice. He looked through the scattered shards, through the ice, into the soldier's face. The soldier looked to his side, then back to the prince. He beat his fist against the ceiling of ice. The soldier tried to maneuver away from whatever he saw, but there was nothing in the void from which to launch himself.

The soldier was grabbed by something Lewin could not see. He began to move. Lewin lost sight of him. Lewin swept his arm out to the side, scattering the shards of metal, throwing the dusting of snow and ash into the air. He caught a glimpse of the soldier. Lewin crawled after him, sweeping the snow, to keep sight of him. The man's unwanted movement sped up and Lewin regained his feet.

He kept his eyes on the man and followed. The soldier looked up at the prince and screamed. He was yanked forward and was lost. Lewin stared unbelieving at the ice and the darkness beneath it.

The wind intensified, assaulting Prince Lewin. Mean-spirited cold found its way through every opening in steel and cloth, biting into his flesh. Lewin searched for cover. He saw the silhouettes of wind-carved red stones through the swirling snow and ash. He ran to the closest large stone and put his back to it. The wind reached him from around the corners. He searched for more effective shelter.

At the base of the next stone he saw the dark elf female. She was standing with her back to the stone, like him. Her furs hid all of her, even hooded her head. Only the ebony skin of her lower face and the bulging, multifaceted eyes of the mask could be seen. She waved for him to approach. He hesitated.

She pointed to a dark pool and yelled. Her voice was lost in the wind. She stepped away from the tower of stone, knelt—her form barely visible in the flurry of snow—and lowered herself into the darkness. Her head and shoulders reappeared. She waved for him, then dropped out of sight.

Prince Lewin knew he could not trust her. He knew she belonged to the enemy. He thought of the soldier under the ice, pulled along by some malevolent force or some unseen creature. He knew he had come to the edge of the desert and that even winter came here, but that did not make sense of this. The dark elf was the enemy, yes, but he realized that he would not last much longer in such harsh, supernatural weather.

He felt for the dagger at his hip, his sword gone, pulled it, and approached the dark pool. As he neared it he could discern that it was a natural opening in the rock. He lowered himself. He stood on a ledge of stone, his eyes adjusted to the feeble light. A dusting of snow settled on the ledge and the floor of the cave. He could not see much more than that. He climbed down, holding the dagger before him. The cave was quieter and calmer than the surface.

"Come," called a female voice from the darkness.

"I can't see."

He heard the striking of flint on stone and saw sparks fall. The head of a torch came alive with flame. The fire was lifted, held aloft. The cave and torchbearer came into view. The cave was small, shaped like an egg on its side, and featureless. The light of the torch disappeared into the mouth of a tunnel behind the dark elf woman. She reached up and pulled the hood down. She slid off the fly mask, revealing eyes that seemed to have been soaked in blood and had taken on that color.

"You need to warm yourself or you'll die," she stated. "Follow me." She turned and entered the tunnel.

Prince Lewin followed her. He wanted to ask her about the snow and ice. He wanted to ask her about the soldier he had seen, even about the strange mask she wore, yet caution held his tongue.

He began to suspect the dark elves had called upon powerful magics, had called on their dark gods, which were demons, if the rumors were true, which had sent the unnatural storm. The dark elf woman must have suspected his thoughts. She turned and looked over her shoulder.

"A strange fate grips you in its icy talons," she stated. Not expecting a response, she turned away from him and continued down the tunnel.

"We've been defeated," said Prince Lewin.

She laughed.

"We underestimated you."

"Obviously."

"Magic?"

She glanced over her shoulder but looked away without answering.

"We were assured that your people weren't disciplined enough to master the complexities of truly dangerous magic, magic of that sort," he glanced behind him, but could no longer see anything outside of the flickering pool of torchlight. "We were wrong."

"Not really," she replied. "Few dark elves manage a true mastery of magic. That sort of thing takes decades of quiet, undisturbed study." She spun. "Violence fills our lives and makes them chaotic and short." She studied him. "How old are you?"

He saw no reason to hide his age. "Sixteen."

"So young." She spun and continued to lead the way down the winding tunnel. The Prince's curiosity overcame him.

"Are we going to Pwyll?" he asked. "Will you ransom me?"

"Ransom?"

"We know your people will not survive the winter. You have no food stores. The citizens of Seven Rivers knew this as well. They feared an attack on their stores, so we came."

"Ah, the citizens of Seven Rivers." She sighed. "Unto them now is the moment of difficult choices."

"What will you do to them?"

"We are not a conquering people. We are a parasitic people," she said, in a matter-of-fact tone.

His concern returned to himself. He continued in the earlier vein. "The King, my father, will empty our granaries to get me back," he boasted with hopeful confidence.

She glanced over her shoulder at him, then looked away without speaking. They walked for awhile.

"I saw something back there I did not understand," said Prince Lewin. "One of my father's men was under the ice. Come to think of it, I saw only horses and your own dead on the surface, none of my father's men. Perchance, were all of the King's men taken under the ice?" The thought caused him to shudder.

She paused. He stopped and looked at her, staring at the pool of darkness at the back of her head. The crackle of the fire echoed off of the stone.

"It's your own fate you should worry about." She turned her head so she could see him and he could see her face. "I can help you."

"What do you mean?"

She faced forward. "Where do you think you are?"

"In a tunnel, approaching Pwyll," he answered, looking at the stone walls and ceiling.

"You've already been to Pwyll," she announced. "You were captured and taken to Maljamir. You were tossed at the feet of the demons. An offering of gratitude, not that they did a damn thing for us." She spun to face him. Her eyes traveled over him. "They began to fight over their prize; young, as you are, with noble features and pure blood. Oh, how they blazed with lust for you. How they wanted to use and hurt you." A wicked smile spread across her face. "Are you a virgin?" He did not answer. She stepped closer to him. He was tall for his age and looked down at her. "I plucked you from their grasp and threw you into Cocytus," she motioned with her head to the snow-blasted desert above. "Out of their reach."

"Cocytus?" He had never heard of such a land. He studied her. He could now see that her smooth ebony skin was marred by open wounds; spots where scabs had been picked free. As he looked at her he noticed a few flies crawl from wound to wound, feeding on her blood. The sores and the activity of the flies seemed not to irritate her.

Her upraised arm held open her cloak. He saw no weapons. He held his dagger between them, emboldening him.

"A deception?" He returned his gaze to her sore-speckled face. "I've been warned against your treachery. There's no need to deceive me. I realize I'm a prisoner. As you said, I have royal blood. I would be best used for trade than for evil sport."

"What's a prince worth?" She chuckled. "In sacks of grain? Casks of ale? You think you'll be ransomed for bacon and bread?" As she spoke one of the flies launched itself from her cheek and buzzed close to his face. He reflexively lifted his free hand and waved it away. He watched as the fly circled back towards its host, spiraled on the updraft from the flame until it finally disappeared from the light. He returned his attention to his strange captor.

"If you're a parasite," he said, "feed."

The smile faded from her face. "You're quite sure of matters, for such a young man," she observed. "I can see you seated with the wisest men your father could compel to teach you. What did you learn from them? Eh? Theories of war? Of rulership? What good has it done you?" She waved her hand. "Here you are. Defeated and alone." She frowned. "That royal blood you boast of has filled you with false confidence."

She half turned and extended the torch. Prince Lewin could see that the tunnel opened into a cave. The ceiling disappeared into darkness. The light of the torch illuminated a rough pyramid of split logs between a pair of fur-lined sleeping pallets. He saw leather packs, various tools and supplies necessary for travel in a cold climate. There was something else, at the edge of light, that he couldn't quite make out. There was movement about it, and an unsettling smell.

The voice of the dark elf captured his attention. "Soon you'll be stripped of all illusions." She looked at him. "You face a truly horrible fate. But, I can save you." She entered the cave and lowered the torch to the split wood. "Just as I saved you from freezing to death."

The logs took the flames from the torch. The cave and tunnel mouth filled with light. She pulled the torch from the fire and held it close to her face, feeling its warmth. "And from," she paused. A sinister grin spread over her face. Her eyes rolled to the side, flashing evil at him, "whatever was under the ice."

The fire light crawled over the strange object at the edge of the camp, as did a multitude of flies. It dawned on Prince Lewin what the misshapen heap was. It was the sword-chopped remains of a fallen soldier. He caught glimpses of white flesh under the thick blanket of flies. Movement interrupted his view of the corpse. His hostess swung the torch violently, extinguishing it.

"What's your name?" asked Prince Lewin as the female dark elf stripped out of her clothing. She did not attempt to hide her nakedness. Just before modesty forced him to avert his gaze he caught a glimpse of the patches of raw, bloody flesh that covered an alarming portion of her body. She crawled into her pile of furs, holding their edges up, allowing flies, leaving their cold-corpse meal for her warm blood, to swarm her naked form. She enclosed herself and the flies in her furs without answering him.

For some time he heard her mumbling over the crackle of the fire and the buzzing of the flies. Her one-sided conversation was accompanied by giggles, moans, and movement under the fur. Eventually, she quieted. He could see the rhythmic rise and fall of her blankets.

He knew he should strip out of his wet clothing and heavy, ice-encrusted armor, and wrap himself in the furs. He did not feel safe enough. He sat on his pallet. He pulled the furs around his legs and waist. His companion was asleep, or seemed to be, and he was exhausted.

He knew he was missing time. He remembered the assault on Pwyll. General Ord had the men and horses working to dislodge the boulders the dark elves had packed into the cave opening, the opening that led to Pwyll. He remembered that the dark elves had attacked, a surprise attack, while the men were unprepared. It was chaos. He had been well away from the assault, just incase, yet he rushed forward, his retinue chasing him. All else seemed a blur and then he awoke in the snow and ice.

If the dark elf was telling the truth much had transpired that he was unaware of. He could not believe it, even though he had felt the cold and seen the soldier under the ice. The talk of demons fighting over him was ludicrous.

Yes, he had been taught by wise scribes and learned men, and yes, even these men said other planes existed whose inhabitants were monsters or worse, yet to think he had left one world and gone to another was simply too much to believe. He had nothing in his experience to match it.

He found his head nodding, eyelids drooping. As wary as he was of the bizarre dark elf, he could no longer stave off exhaustion. He stretched out on his side, pulled the furs on top of him, and closed his eyes.

. . .

"Prince Lewin!" a voice yelled. He opened his eyes and sat up. All was dark. He realized that he was not under the furs. Nor was he in his armor, for the weight and chill of it was absent. He felt around him. He was on a floor of stone, as before, but there was nothing padding his sleep nor covering him. He felt his person and discovered only rags.

"Prince Lewin!" called a man's voice. Lewin became aware of a rectangle of light hovering on the wall across from him. He stood and was now eye-level with the light. He felt around him in the darkness as he approached it. He discerned it was a small glassless window through which candle-light shone. He peered through and saw the face of a male dark elf.

"Prince Lewin, give me your hand," the dark elf commanded.

"What?" he asked, confused. "Where am I? What's happened?"

"Give me your hand."

"I was in a cave," protested Lewin. "There was a woman."

The candle was snuffed out. Darkness pressed in on all sides. "Wait! Wait, please."

The candle was re-lit. Prince Lewin saw the male dark elf.

"Give me your hand."

"What are you going to do?" asked Lewin.

"Place food in it."

At the mention of food Lewin's stomach began to ache. He hesitantly reached through the window. The dark elf male set the candle down. The light of the candle was joined by a second, less vibrant light. He felt his wrist grasped and held tight. A red-orange glow approached his hand. He realized it was a hot coal and tried to wrench his wrist free but it was too late. The hot coal, held by tongs, was dropped onto his palm. The dark elf dropped the tongs, which clattered on the stone, and, with his own fingers, closed Lewin's fingers around the coal. The male laughed, as Lewin struggled to open his hand and pull his wrist free.

Lewin screamed as the searing heat of the coal burned his palm and fingers. He worked his arm against the wooden edges of the opening, scraping and bruising the flesh of his forearm, but he did not register the additional pain. The burning of the coal reached down into his arm with fiery roots. The laughter of the male crescendoed.

The coal was cooling and the male grew tired of his evil sport. He released the prince's hand and wrist. Lewin dropped the offensive item and pulled his hand back through the opening.

"Smell that cooking flesh?" asked the male. "Dinner is served." He laughed, putting out the candle.

Lewin staggered backwards into the darkness, gripping his wrist, holding his hand in front of his face, although he couldn't see it.

"You trusted him?" asked an unexpected voice. He turned, peering into the darkness. He had not realized there was a second prisoner in the cell with him.

"What?"

"Did you really believe he was going to give you food?"

He recognized the voice. "You!" He backed into the wall and slumped down, holding his injured hand between his thighs.

"Let me see your hand."

"How can you see anything at all?" he shot back. He felt foolish and vulnerable at having trusted the male dark elf. He also felt disoriented and afraid. He had fallen asleep in the cave and woke up in a cell. He figured the female dark elf had somehow hastened his capture and confinement, yet here she was, in the cell with him.

"I'm a dark elf," she said. He could hear her movements. "Don't blame yourself," she added. "You have no idea the tricks they'll play. You haven't learned how to guard yourself against them." She was next to him now. She touched his upper arm. "Let me see."

"Did you press foul roots against my lips as I slept, robbing me of my wits?" he asked. "Or use magic to deepen my slumber so you could transport me here?"

"What?"

"We were in the cave. You said you could save me and yet here you have delivered me to captivity."

"You're delirious," she said. "You've been feverish, tossing and turning, ever since you were thrown in here with me. This is the first we've spoken." She reached for his forearm and gently pried his hand out of the protection of his legs. She held his wrist and looked at his hand. Lewin could not see her, only feel her touch and hear her voice.

"You defeated our army with magic, calling a blizzard to bury our soldiers and horses." He turned to her in the darkness. "You even caught your own soldiers in the ice, but cared not."

"There was a fair coating of ash on that coal." She let go of his wrist. "You were fortunate."

"Fortunate?" he shot back at her. He was going to continue his complaint but she spoke over him.

"You certainly did lose the battle, but I have no idea what magic you're talking about. I don't hear much down here, but I've overheard the guards bragging about the battle and the rather simple deception you fell for." He heard her scoot away. "I have some food. There must be plenty now, if they're feeding *me*."

He could tell by the shape of her voice that she was turned away. She scooted back to him, touched his arm, and said, "give me your *other* hand." She couldn't help but snicker when she said this. He held up his unburned hand and she placed something tough and dense in it. "Horse flesh."

"Do you know what happened to me?" he asked as he sniffed the meat. He was hungry but he didn't feel secure eating the meat. Still, he held onto it.

"I know you're Prince Lewin, now I do, anyway. I know you are the only human brought down here so far. I know you just held onto a hot coal and now you're holding onto horse meat, which you're not eating." She paused. "That's all I know about you."

"You lie!" he countered. "We met on the surface. You led me out of the blizzard, into a cave. Now you've brought me here. What I don't understand is why you're in here with me, another deception?"

"Another prisoner."

"You said that you could save me from a horrible fate," he accused her.

"Eat the meat and try to get some rest," she said, scooting away from him. Reminded of the meat, he found the solution to his growing hunger harder and harder to resist. He nibbled on the meat and tried to piece together the unbelievable events that had happened to him. Despite the cold and his discomfort, the come-down from the pain made him sleepy. Once his body began digesting the meat he was unable to stay awake.

. . .

The sounds of a thousand flies buzzing furiously about him stirred Prince Lewin from his slumber. He once more felt the soft comfort of fur against his skin. He sat up with a jolt and threw the furs off of him. He felt for his dagger, found it, and held it out. His eyes adjusted to the dim light. Little remained of the fire but burnt ends and a hill of ash, which had been spilled as the logs collapsed.

The female dark elf was sitting behind the soldier's corpse. She was as he had first seen her, in her pose of prayer, mask covering her eyes, forearms coated in congealed blood, the flies feeding. She mumbled to herself, head bent.

Lewin gathered himself into a crouch. He was in his armor. His clothing was stiff but dry. He glanced around the cave, spotting the leather bags, tools, and gear. He also saw a short spear leaned against the stone wall. He stood and made his way to the spear. He sheathed his dagger and grabbed the spear. He approached the praying dark elf and pressed the point of the spear just between her breasts.

"What's your name, witch?"

She looked up at him through the fly-eyed mask, but said nothing. He bent forward and reached for the mask. Grabbing it, he yanked it from her head and tossed it to the floor. It clattered to a stop. He regained a two-handed grip on the spear. "You're the source of the blizzard. You used magic to twist my dreams into nightmares. You let these flies feed on your blood. What kind of sorceress are you?" He shook his head, not expecting, or even wanting, an answer. "I wish we had destroyed your city and your foul race!"

She regarded him with her blood-swamped eyes and said nothing. He held the spear in place with one hand and reached down with the other. He began to unbuckle his belt. The dark elf moved her eyes, watching. A queer smile came to her face.

A terrible pain struck Lewin as he worked the belt free. He pulled his hand back and looked at it. The flesh of his palm and the pads of his fingers were blistered. He stared at his hand in disbelief.

"You flail in your sleep," said the dark elf. He looked at her. "You struck the fire."

"Lies," he whispered. "Hold out your wrists."

She did as she was told. He realized the absurdity of his command when he saw her gore and fly covered hands, wrists, and forearms. He knew the belt would slip. "Damn you, witch."

"I've already been to Hell," she said, smirking.

He bent forward, yanked the spear, and struck her in the side of the head with the wooden shaft. "Don't speak!" he yelled. "Dream twister! Fly mother! No more foul magic will cross your lips." He replaced the tip of the spear between her breasts. "Wipe the blood free."

She bent one hand towards the other, prompting him to dig the tip of the spear through the cloth of her shirt, into her flesh, lest she get ideas. With slow movements the dark elf cleaned her arms of the congealed blood. The flies swarmed and buzzed, upset by the disturbance.

He bent, and, keeping the spear against her as best he could, bound her wrists with his belt. He knew it was a haphazard restraint, especially given the slimy residue still on her skin, but it was something. He stood. "I'm taking you prisoner."

She chuckled.

He pressed the spear into her enough to halt her laughter. "It's good you brought gear. We're going to the surface. We'll make our way to Seven Rivers. I'll hold you hostage, should we come across any of your kind. Now get up." He pulled the spear back far enough for her to rise.

"Oh, foolish boy," she began. He stepped forward, spun the spear, and slammed the butt of it into her stomach. She doubled over in pain, gasping for air.

"No talking."

"Eideothea," she spat out.

For a moment Lewin feared she had spoke some foul word of power. He tensed, expecting black magic. The dark elf female rose, touching her stomach. "My name is Eideothea."

. . .

Prince Lewin kept his captive at spear point. He commanded her to gather the gear. He commanded her to relight the torch in the coals of the fire. After that, he nodded towards the tunnel and she took the lead.

"It doesn't go—" she started but the spear tip jabbed her in the small of the back, silencing her. She stepped quickly, pulling herself from the point. She mumbled the rest of her warning, "where you think it goes," but he didn't hear her. The pair began down the winding tunnel. "Seven Rivers may not even exist anymore," she observed. Prince Lewin struck her in the side of her head with the flat of the spear blade. "Ow," She reached up and touched her ear.

"No talking, witch," said Lewin. "You'll weave your spells between common words."

"I'm simply pointing out—" Again the spear. She stumbled to the side. She felt the cut on her ear and the warm blood dripping from it. The flies, tired of old wounds, took flight and followed the aroma of fresh blood. "You debase yourself, treating me cruelly," she admonished Prince Lewin. He prodded her with the spear, but with less enthusiasm. "I might also point out—"

Prince Lewin grabbed the flap of the leather satchel strung over her shoulder and yanked her to a stop. He reached over her shoulder and grabbed the front of her shirt. He pushed her to the side until she struck the tunnel wall. He pressed his fist against her chest.

"You don't need your tongue to be a valuable hostage."

Eideothea looked up at the prince. She studied the nobility of his features. She relished the stern set to his mouth and eyes. Such strength appealed to her. Prince Lewin gleamed some understanding of her thinking. Confusion jumbled his features, then disgust. He began to release the Eideothea, but was forced to keep his grip as she spoke aloud her thinking.

"I'm not loved among my kind. Even if I was, you should know, that if a dark elf is taken hostage and used as leverage." She looked into his eyes. "The first thing we do is kill the hostage, then we kill the hostage taker." She lifted her non-torch holding hand and traced her fingers along the back of his fist, feeling the raised tendons. "Long negotiations bore us."

Lewin yanked his hand free from her touch. "Does the sickness of your people know no limit?" He turned his head. "Walk."

Eideothea pushed herself from the wall, turned, glancing at Lewin, and continued down the tunnel. "You never answered me."

"Will you never cease talking?"

She glanced over her shoulder. "Are you a virgin?" she asked. Lewin's eyes hardened.

When they reached the egg-shaped cave Lewin grabbed her shoulder. He peered past her. A shaft of blue-white light came through the opening. He prodded her forward with the spear tip. When they were below the opening he peered up into the light and snow. Eideothea looked at him.

"You'll have to decide," she said.

He turned to face her. The movement of the flies on her ear caught his attention. He glanced at them then looked back into her face. She started to continue her proposition but he surprised her. He reached out and covered her mouth with one hand. He leaned the spear against the wall then grabbed the torch from her. He lifted the torch and thrust the head into the bank of snow above.

She watched him with her blood-washed eyes. He reached without turning his eyes from her and drew his dagger.

"I'm going to remove my hand," he said. "If you open your mouth you'll find a dagger in it." He looked at her. He pulled his hand back. She looked at him, studying him. He cut free a length of cloth from his tabard. He sheathed his dagger and grabbed the back of her head, bending it forward. Eideothea knew he intended to gag her.

Before he could, she blurted out, "Wear the furs."

He paused.

"You're not dressed for the cold," she explained. He smiled, shaking his head in disbelief.

"Thanks."

"You're welcome." She opened her mouth in preparation for the gag.

He shook his head in disbelief as he placed the cloth between her teeth and tied it behind her head. The flies on her ears lifted into flight and danced around the movement of his arms. He spun her around to face away from him. He pulled the furs free from their bindings and dressed as she had advised. He spun her back around. She watched him as he checked the belt, then tightened the knot.

He looked up out of the opening. "When will this unnatural storm end?"

'Never,' she thought.

Prince Lewin looked to her, saw the gag, and smiled at his quick forgetfulness. He reached out and grabbed her left arm above the elbow. He helped her onto the ledge and then boosted her to the surface. He followed with the spear in-hand. The wind was awaiting their arrival and blew with fury to greet them.

Lewin marched through the shin-high snow, head bent against the wind, dragging the dark elf female behind him. When he felt he had gone far enough out into the open, he shielded his eyes and looked around. He did not see the entrance to Pwyll. For a moment he thought it might have disappeared under ice and snow but there was nothing but a featureless white plain where he expected sloping, rocky hills.

He turned and looked in the direction of Seven Rivers. Even on a clear day he would have only been able to make out its shapes and tones but his vision was diminished by the blowing snow. Still, somehow, the land did not slope as he expected but extended out level. He turned and looked, he thought, up the foothills of the Black Ogre Mountains. He expected to see snow-topped boulders and wind-shaped stone towers but once again the featureless white plain extended.

He looked all around him. There was only white and wind. He felt disoriented and with that, he felt fear. He thought to retreat to the cave, yank Eideothea's gag, and make the witch end her hellish spell. He searched for their footprints, found them, then pulled the dark elf into motion. He followed the trail to its termination but the cave entrance could not be seen.

"What?" he asked, astonished. He released the dark elf and knelt down in the snow. He began to search the snow for the cave entrance. Finding nothing he turned to Eideothea. "Where—" But she was gone. He regained his feet and looked all around. There was no sight of the dark elf. He looked to the snow. The wind, gusting, erased their tracks. It was as if he had been dropped in this very spot.

Having no feature to place his hope on, no direction being any more promising than any other, Prince Lewin chose to head towards where he believed Seven Rivers to be. He could not trust his senses, he thought, but perhaps he could trust his feet.

Prince Lewin was strong, disciplined, and even had the benefit of furs, but no man can long stand the frozen plain, the relentless assault of the wind, and the omnipresent cold. He was half-unconscious when he finally collapsed.

. . .

Eideothea caught up to Lewin, leaving his belt and gag far behind in the snow. She dropped to her knees next to him. She rolled him onto his back, so that his face was no longer buried in the snow. She understood the cold and how to endure it. She knew Lewin was in danger. She dropped the packs from her shoulders, pulled one in front of her, and began to dig amongst the tools.

She pulled a folded, saw-toothed blade free and unfolded it, locking it in place with a pin. She rose and stepped to the side. She bent and began to saw the thick floor of snow into blocks. These she stacked as she went along, forming a circular wall around Lewin's unconscious body.

"You—," muttered Lewin.

Eideothea turned from the cutting, set the saw down, and knelt over him.

"You—" he repeated. He stirred and tried to sit up but collapsed back onto the snow.

She leaned closer to him and intended to comfort him with her words but he surprised her. He reached up and grabbed the collar of her fur cloak. He yanked against her and brought himself up, smashing his forehead against her face. The blow forced her from his grasp. She doubled over backwards.

Prince Lewin rolled over and began to crawl away from the dark elf. He tried to stand, crashed through an unexpected low wall of snow, and faltered. Snow flew from the shattered blocks and blinded him. He stopped and shook his head, casting off the snowy mask. This made him dizzy. The bright white of the trackless plain faded to darkness. He felt the blood run from his head. His legs failed him. Once again, he was face down in the snow.

Eideothea reached up and touched her face. When she pulled her hand back there was fresh blood. She could feel her left eye swelling shut. The blow, so unexpected and hard, stirred stars in her vision. Still, being a dark elf, she had been struck in the face many times. She knew she had to think past the pain.

She pictured the spear and Lewin rising over her to drive it home. This forced her into action. She rolled onto her side and looked for Lewin. When she saw him lying face-down in the snow she calmed. She allowed herself a moment to nurse her pain, resting the injured side of her face on the snow. For a few moments the cold forced the pain and swelling away. Then it introduced its own hurt.

She stood and walked to Lewin. She turned him over once again, picked up the saw, and began to cut fresh blocks. He did not stir again as she completed the domed shelter of snow. She crouched in the snow and stripped herself bare. The flies she had been sheltering flew about, exploring the space and the fresh cut along her cheekbone. She used her furs to make a pallet.

She bent over Lewin, opened his furs and stripped him. She crawled on top of him and pulled her own furs over them to trap their shared heat. She worked her hands slowly over his chilled flesh, using friction to work the life-heat back into him. He stirred and muttered half-formed words from the edge of consciousness.

"Shhh, you're at death's door, my valiant prince. Don't enter that bleak house."

The flies buzzed in the air above them. Eideothea snaked her arm through the furs, forming a little tunnel of entrance. When the flies saw her ebony-skinned hand against the backdrop of white they swarmed together and angled their flight to her. They crawled down the familiar flesh of her arm onto her shoulder and breasts. They found in that dark, warm shelter a new body. They began to explore it with curiosity.

"Baalzebul favors you," she whispered into his ear. "Do you feel his caress?" He moaned, recognizing her presence and touch, but was not cognizant of her words. "Accept his charity. Accept his truth," she advised. "Baalzebul," she said in reverent tones, "Lord of the Seventh, Hell's greatest Angel, He Who is Victorious. Accept him. Accept him." Her litany wove itself into his mind as he drifted deeper into unconsciousness.

. . .

The sound of the rusty hinges woke him. He opened his eyes. A dark elf male stood in the doorway, lit by candlelight. Prince Lewin looked around the cell and found her. She was curled up against the wall. He could barely make out her shape in the feeble light.

"Stop it!" he screamed at her. "End your spell, witch!" She woke and half turned. The dark elf male stepped into the room, laughing.

"What do you want from me?" asked Prince Lewin, directing his question to Eideothea. She looked at him, then turned her eyes to the dark elf male. Lewin saw a look of alarm cross her features. He looked at the guard, just in time to see the man motion towards the door. Several other guards rushed into the cell.

One guard stood in front of Lewin, a short sword in his hand, pointed at the prince. Two other guards went to Eideothea. Knowing what was coming, she curled up in a defensive ball. The guards began kicking her. One reached down and began to pry her out of her clenched position. He rolled her onto her back, knelt on top of her, pinning her down with a knee in her gut, and held her arms apart. He said something to his companion in the dark elf language. The second guard bent forward and struck

Eideothea in the face. She turned her head, trying to shield herself, as he hit her again.

"What are you doing?" cried Prince Lewin. "Stop! Leave her alone!" He reflexively moved toward her. The dark elf with the short sword growled at him and pressed the tip of the sword against his chest.

"Stop what? We aren't doing anything?" argued the male guard with the candle.

Lewin looked to him. "You're beating her! Why?"

The sounds of violence filled the small cell; the grunting of the men, the thuds of their boots and fists on Eideothea's unprotected body, her cries of pain.

The dark elf guard with the candle stepped closer to Lewin. "You're doing this!" he screamed. "You have the gall to blame us, when it's you who reject him?"

"Who?" cried Lewin.

Eideothea screamed as the guards struck her.

"Enough!" said the guard. "You'll kill her. He doesn't want that, not yet, not unless she fails." The guards beating Eideothea stood panting over her. She curled up, not in defense, but in pain. Her agonized moaning undercut the guard's words.

"Look what you've done by rejecting him." The guard shook his head as the other men passed behind him, exiting the cell. "Like any father, he can be merciful," said the male. "All he asks for is love and devotion." The male backed towards the door. "When you spurn him, when you deny his love, when the child fails the father, what's left?" He glanced towards Eideothea. "Wrath." He blew out the candle and shut the door.

Lewin crawled to Eideothea. He reached out and touched her. She had stopped moaning. "Eideothea?" He wasn't sure why he had concern for her. Perhaps, he thought, it was the suddenness and violence of the unexpected attack that called upon his natural empathy

28

and concern for others. "Eideothea? Are you—" But he needn't finish his question. She couldn't hear him. She had passed out from the pain.

He lay next to her and placed a protective arm around her. "I won't let them do that again," he whispered to her. He held her until exhaustion took him.

. . .

Prince Lewin tossed and turned. He was hot. There was pressure on him. There was a nuisance on his flesh. He struggled to awaken. He felt pain and hunger. These sharp things stirred him.

"Shhh, Prince," whispered Eideothea. She rest her head next to his, her face turned to him. Her lips caressed the skin of his neck as she spoke. He let the warm, soft presence push him back into the peace and quiet of sleep.

. . .

Prince Lewin awoke in the darkness. He was cold and shivering. He was holding something, 'no, someone,' he realized. The darkness was total but he knew from touch he was holding Eideothea. His left arm was trapped beneath her waist and the stone floor. He pulled it free and used his elbow to prop himself up.

'The cell,' he thought.

He could feel the rags he wore. Gone were the furs. He began to disentangle his right arm from Eideothea's crossed-arm-grip. She stirred and pulled his arm against her, mumbling something in her native tongue. He paused his movement, feeling a twang of guilt at the prospect of waking her. He frowned at his own thinking. He yanked his arm free and scooted away from her. He sat with his back against the wall. He could hear her legs move, scrapping the floor, as she curled up in an attempt to keep hold of the shared warmth.

"When will you end this nightmare?" he asked. She moved in the darkness. "Do you delight in being both the cause of, and partner to, my misery?"

"I told you—"

"Yes, you can save me," he interrupted. "You also said you had taken me to Cocytus, where neither dark elf nor demon could find me."

"—I'm a fellow prisoner," she finished.

"Prince Lewin!"

The candlelight reappeared in the small rectangular slot in the door. The male looked through the opening. "Move to the wall, away from the other prisoner."

Lewin heard the jangle of keys. He heard the scrape of the iron bar. The door opened. The dark elf male stepped into the cell. Lewin thought to charge him, to tackle him and beat him into unconsciousness.

"Get up!" the dark elf yelled. He grabbed Lewin by the arm and lifted him to his feet. Lewin found that it was difficult to keep his balance. Without the jailer's "help," he would have fallen, weakened by hunger, fatigue, and stress. The dark elf drug him to the wall of the cell, pressed his back against the stone.

Eideothea turned her face into the candlelight. Lewin saw that the entire left side of her face was swollen. The flesh around her left eye was puffy. A dull red scab extended down the ridge of her cheek bone.

The guard brought his face close to Lewin's. "If you try to interfere, it will be much worse."

Lewin looked into the male's face. He shifted his gaze to a pair of males that entered the cell through the open door. The second male to enter was pulling on a pair of skin-tight gloves.

"Strip her," commanded the male with the candle.

"What are you—" began Lewin.

The dark elf guard smiled. "Show him."

The male with the gloves turned and stepped up to Lewin. The other male cornered Eideothea and began to grab at her rags, despite her protest and scrambling. Lewin looked from the guard with the candle to the struggle in the corner.

The gloved guard brought his hands, palm up, into view. Something sparkled in the candle light on the palm and fingers of his gloves. Lewin looked down. Dozens of metal shards pierced the skin of each glove. The guard smiled and lowered his hands. "You're going to flay her." Said the guard with the candle.

"Me?" gasped Lewin.

"It's because you reject him," argued the guard. "He lashes out because he's hurt. This is your doing."

The two guards ripped the rags from Eideothea. The bare-handed guard lifted to her feet and held her immobile, arms pinned behind her back. The jutting bones of her emaciated body reflected the candlelight in glowing, angular planes. The shard-gloved guard stood in front of her, palms out.

"Don't!" cried Lewin. He pushed against the guard restraining him. The guard dropped his arm. A dagger hidden in his sleeve fell into his hand. He pressed the point into Lewin's abdomen. "I'll gut you."

Lewin tried to twist to the side, but the dagger dug into his flesh. He paused and looked into the guard's face. The high cheekbones and narrow jaw caught the flickering light, giving the face a hard-edged appearance, as if his features were not composed of curved forms, but of steel, like the shards in the flaying gloves.

"Then we'll have our fun with her."

A cry from Eideothea caught Lewin's attention. He looked from the guard to her.

The shard-gloved guard stepped forward. He grabbed her breasts with his hands and squeezed them. As

Lewin watched he clinched his hands into fists. He yanked his hands towards his hips. Eideothea tried to bend with his movement but the guard holding her pulled her erect. Even in the weak light, Lewin saw blood spray against the wall, floor, and gloved guard. Lewin looked away.

"No, no, that won't do," muttered the guard pinning him against the wall with his dagger. "You need to watch."

"I won't be witness to your cruelty," countered Lewin. "Nor am I the cause of it!"

"You'll watch," said the male in a low voice. "Or we will flay every piece of skin from her and leave her in your arms to die."

Lewin returned his eyes to Eideothea. The candlelight reflected off of the slick of blood traveling downwards from the valley between her breasts to the edge of her concave stomach.

The gloved guard reached down with his right hand, sliding his fingers against Eideothea's pubic mound. She pressed her thighs together to prevent him from moving his hand lower. The guard behind her began to work his knee between her thighs from behind. The gloved guard laughed, placed his palms against her thighs, and drug the shards of metal across her unprotected skin. She cried out in pain.

"Enough!" screamed Lewin. "Enough! What do you want?" The gloved guard paused his movement. Lewin looked to the guard pinning him to the wall. "You want me to accept him? Is that it? I accept! Do you hear me? I accept? I accept."

"Do you now?" purred the guard. He glanced over his shoulder. "Did I tell you to stop?"

Lewin brought his arm across his body, knocking the dark elf's hand, and the dagger it held, to the side. He pushed himself from the wall and dodged past the startled guard. The two dark elves tormenting Eideothea turned and looked. Lewin rushed the man with the gloves. He swung at him. The guard twisted to the side, evading the blow, but Lewin's momentum carried him into the guard. The two men slammed into the stone wall.

The second guard threw Eideothea to the floor and stepped over her. As Lewin and the gloved guard tangled their arms and bodies, the second guard grabbed Lewin's shoulder from behind. He half spun the prince, partially extracting him from his wild grapple. Lewin turned his face just in time to meet the fist coming at him. He saw stars, then darkness.

. . .

"Lewin! Wake up!"

He opened his eyes and looked into Eideothea's face. She was holding up the edge of the furs, letting light in. He could see that the swelling on the left side of her face had gone down. She had, however, picked the scab from the cut on her cheek. Several flies lined the edges, drinking.

Lewin became aware that he was naked, that she was naked on top of him, and that flies were crawling back and forth on their exposed flesh. He tried to disentangle himself from her, to find his way out of the furs. He paused his frantic actions as memories flooded over him.

"The cell," he breathed. "They were flaying you. I —" He glanced down at her breasts but could not see them. They were pressed against his chest and hidden by shadow. He again began to squirm out from under her.

"Don't," she advised him. "This is the only way to stay warm." She lowered the edge of the furs. Only a dim glow crept into their cocoon. "You've were mostly dead, then, eventually, half alive." She smiled, "I saved you from freezing to death—again."

"The cell?"

33

"Fever dream."

He looked at her in the gloom. "Cocytus?"

"Yes."

"There is no cell?" he asked. "No dark elves tormenting us?"

"You are far from Pwyll."

"I dream of it?" he asked, more of himself than her. "So real," he whispered. "I was in a cell." He studied her face in the gloom. "We were in a cell. It's too real to be a dream. Your face." He realized his hand was against her body. He felt the pain of the puffy blisters on his palm. "The burn on my hand, from the coal."

"From the logs."

"Let me see your breasts, your thighs," he demanded.

She turned her face from his.

"If you have cuts—" His voice trailed. He realized that he didn't know what it would mean if she had cuts. 'Would it mean that *this* is the dream?' he asked himself.

"You have to eat and drink," she advised. "You've been standing at death's door."

"Which is real?" he asked. "Which is real and which is the lie? They can't both be true." She began to rise. He tried to grip her, hold her in place, but she was slippery with sweat. She rose into a crouch, spinning away from him, pulling the fur around her. Lewin at once felt the chill air attack his skin.

He rose into a crouch and began to pull the winter wear into place. As he did so he noticed a wash of blood on his chest. He looked over his body. He saw that his thighs were also pink with the mixture of blood and sweat. Then he noticed it. The red divot in his abdomen. 'The guard's dagger,' he thought.

"Look at me," he commanded Eideothea.

She paused in her dressing and looked over her shoulder.

"This wound." He glanced down at his stomach. He looked back to her. "The guard's dagger."

Eideothea turned away. She pulled the furs into place. "I have rations and water. We have to eat, then we have to move."

"I'm not going anywhere."

"Then you'll die on the frozen plain." She turned on her knees to face him. The cloud of flies buzzed around the pair.

Lewin stared into her blood-filled eyes.

"I accepted him," he stated. "I told the guard that I accepted him, so they would stop hurting you."

Eideothea studied his face, without speaking.

"Let me see your breasts," he said, his voice gentler then before. "If you don't, I won't trust you. I won't travel with you. I'll take my chances."

"You'll die."

"Then I'll die."

Eideothea frowned. "I didn't know humans were so stubborn." She reached up and pulled open her furs, exposing her breasts. Lewin looked from her large, blood-washed eyes, to her small, pert breasts. They too were washed with blood. Scores of parallel red cuts seeped blood. As he studied her breasts, blood ran to her cold-erected nipples, formed twin teardrops, and fell onto the fur.

"The cell is real," murmured Lewin. "This is the lie." He looked into her face. "The guard did that. I saw it happen."

Eideothea closed her fur coat. "No," she countered. "I did this to myself." She studied him. "You were on the edge of death. You were feverish and delirious, but you were still aware enough to notice my actions, on some

35

level." She paused, studying him. "If there is a deception it is you deceiving yourself."

"Why?" he asked. "Why would you do that to yourself?"

A slow smile crossed her face. "For you."

He looked at her, not understanding.

"So he would show you kindness."

"Who?" he asked.

"My master."

"Who is your master?"

"Baalzebul, the Lord of Flies. He fed on my blood. He accepted my offering. Death did *not* take you."

"A lie!" His anger filled the small, domed space. He lowered his voice to a harsh whisper. "I have the guard's cut."

"I did that to you."

"You lie!"

She looked into his eyes. "Our blood had to mingle; he had to taste you, taste us, before he would agree. I used your dagger. Look at it."

He dug through his furs and found his dagger sheath. He pulled the blade free and looked at the tip. The metal was rose-colored. He looked from the dagger to her, then back to the tip of the blade. He was uncertain. 'Is this from before? From her?' He asked himself. He tried to recall if he had drawn her blood. If he had, he tried to recall if he had wiped the blade clean. He could not remember.

"A trick," he whispered.

"For what purpose?" She reached out and touched his hand. Her flesh was warm. He looked down. He was struck by the sharp contrast of her ebony skin at the center of so much whiteness, his own skin, and the background of snow and ice. "I helped you. Just as you helped me," she said. He looked up at her. "You said you negotiated with the guards, gave them what they wanted, to end my suffering."

"You say that isn't real."

"The sentiment is the same. The self-sacrifice." She smiled, looking down at her own chest.

"Is that how you—" He looked into her scabbed face, her red eyes. "Saved me from my horrible fate? By mingling our blood and offering it to, what's his name, Baalzebul?"

"We need to eat," she said, "then move, before a blizzard overtakes us. What the ice takes, the ice keeps."

"Is there no where safe?"

"Yes."

"Where?"

"My master's house."

. . .

Eideothea knocked open the exit of the igloo and crawled out. Prince Lewin followed. The frozen plain extended to the horizon in three directions. In the fourth, a ridge of ice and stone rose from snow to sky. There was little wind, the blizzard had ended while they slept, but the sky swirled with towering, grey-bottomed clouds.

Eideothea helped him to his feet. "Do you want to gag me?" she asked. "Or bind me?" she added, playfully. Lewin looked at her as he pulled up his fur hood. "Maybe you want the spear again?" She smiled as she pulled her fly-eyed goggles into place. She picked up the pack and slung it over her shoulder. She turned and headed towards the rise of ice and stone.

Despite the threatening skies there was little wind. The ground was ice with a dusting of snow. This made every step a hazard yet the pair, under Eideothea's leadership, kept a good pace. The rations, salted meat and a biscuit as hard as stone, keep his hunger pangs at bay.

Lewin kept his head bent down, his eyes squinted against the glare, and focused his attention on Eideothea's footfalls. He walked where she walked.

"There's many types of snow," she said, speaking over her shoulder. "The surface, I mean. It all depends on the humidity, the temperature, the wind. Some snow is easier to walk on than other types. We're lucky, this isn't bad. I've...."

As she spoke his mind wandered. He thought of the cell, of their shared captivity and torture. He asked himself if it was real. He replayed every memory he had since waking up in the snow. He attempted to sort out what was real and what must be deception. He studied Eideothea's face, the inflection of her words, searching for falsehood or truth.

Despite all of his attempts nothing seemed completely real or trustworthy. Soon his physical fatigue returned, as did his hunger. His investigations became an activity he could not afford. He bent all of his energies to lifting one foot and then the other. He realized, after an indeterminable amount of time following Eideothea through the white-on-white terrain, that he had come to depend on her, more than that, he needed her to survive.

. . .

Ice and stone rose sharply in front of them. Eideothea guided him into a steep, blue-walled crevasse in the ice. She seemed to know the terrain. She turned from the initial ravine into a second crevasse that branched from the first. Here she sat on a rock gripped by the ice and rested. He sat next to her.

Blue walls of ice rose in front of and behind them. The ice held massive black stones in its eternal grip. The sky above was filled with various shades of blue, ranging from pale, milky blue to black. Over this backdrop rode puffy white clouds with grey bottoms. Overall, however, the light had not changed.

"How long until nightfall?" he asked.

She was digging in the pack and did not answer. She pulled out more rations and divided them between them. She produced a water skin from deep within the folds of her furs, where it was kept from freezing. "There's no day or night here. It is always thus." She lifted and hand to her goggles, raised them to her forehead, and glanced up at the sky.

He looked from her to the sky. He saw no sun, no concentration of light in the sky. "Cocytus," he said, looking around. He studied the ice and stones. "Is this really Hell, as you say?"

She nodded.

"Hell is fire and burning," he protested.

"Cold burns," she stated between chews. "Drink." She handed him the water skin.

"You've been here before?"

She nodded.

"You worship a devil?" He took the water skin, pulled the cap, lifted it to his lips, and poured the rapidly cooling water into his parched mouth.

"Most dark elves worship demons, from the Abyss." She took the water skin back from his extended hand and tucked it back into her furs.

"I don't know the difference."

She shrugged her shoulders. "It's not worth troubling over."

"You want me to accept your master, a devil?"

She looked sidelong at him. "You said you already had." She winked at him, her ebony eyelid, with its white eyelashes, flashed over her blood red eye. Lewin was struck by the oddity of it.

"I—"

"Don't worry, an oath made in duress, or," she looked away from him, "in an altered state, is not a binding oath."

He began to inquire about the cell, about the captivity. It seemed so real, and in it she was present, so it followed she could answer to the particulars. He stopped, realizing she would know nothing other than what he had told her. 'That is,' he concluded, 'if she is to be believed.' He looked from her to the ice and rock. 'If *this* is to be believed.'

Eideothea stood. She pulled the spear from its resting place on the stone and held it out in front of her, towards the entrance to the crevasse. Her body was tense, ready for action. He reached into his furs, finding the dagger. A shadow fell over the opening. Lewin turned.

A massive creature appeared. It clung to the ice at the top of the crevasse, being too large to squeeze itself lower. Both Eideothea and Lewin looked up at it. The creature was unlike anything Lewin had ever seen. At first glance it appeared to be an enormous insect, something like a praying mantis. As he studied it the differences became apparent.

It clung to the ice with two sets of jointed legs that ended in single claws. Like a praying mantis, its frontmost pair of legs folded down, allowing it to grapple its prey. Its abdomen and thorax were covered with thick white fur that completely coated and hid its cuticle plates. The thorax was elongated and jointed so that the creature could hold its fore-body erect. It tilted its head and looked at them with twin, compound eyes.

Lewin saw movement at the periphery of his vision. He glanced and saw Eideothea lower her compound eyed goggles into place. Lewin looked back to the creature above them. It tilted its head and regarded

Eideothea. Or so it appeared, without pupils, it was difficult to tell where it was focusing its attention.

The creature, 'It must be nearly twenty feet long,' thought Lewin, began to click its mandibles. The sound echoed off of the ice. Lewin heard a second clicking, although softer than the first. He realized it was Eideothea and looked at her. She was mimicking the sound. The creature seemed satisfied with her response and began to crawl back into the wider crevasse from which it came.

"Are we—"

"Come on," commanded Eideothea. She grabbed Lewin by the arm and pulled him to his feet.

"We're not going with that—thing?"

"Yes." Eideothea watched both her footing and the creature above them.

"By the gods, what is it?"

"A gelugon," she whispered. "Powerful," she added, with awe.

Lewin leaned in, whispering in her ear. "It's massive."

She glanced from the gelugon to Lewin. A wry smile spread over her face. "Its rather small, for a gelugon." She raised a finger to her lips, indicating Lewin should restrain from any further comments or questions.

The gelugon led them through the maze of broken ice. Finally, it arrived at the edge of the glacier. The crevasse terminated at a towering wall of black stone. The gelugon climbed from the ice to the stone, disappearing over the top. Eideothea knelt and dropped the pack from her shoulders.

"Now what?"

"We climb." Eideothea opened the pack and pulled two pairs of crampons free. These were followed by something like small picks. "Are you afraid of heights?" she asked, looking up.

Lewin looked from the tools to the sheer wall. "What if I am?" he asked, his voice hollow. Eideothea chuckled. She sat and began to strap the crampons to her boots.

. . .

The gelugon was waiting for them at the top. As Eideothea helped pull Lewin over the edge he glanced up at the towering insect. He wished he hadn't. He scooted away from the edge, closer to the gelugon, and began to remove his crampons. The gelugon clicked and Eideothea responded. Their conversation went on for some time, as if they were debating something.

Lewin could see little of the plateau past the gelugon's body. He turned and looked out over the glacier, then past it, to the plain below. He realized that the plain was actually a frozen lake, or even, perhaps, a sea. Until he saw the vast expanse, he had been consoling himself that he was still outside of Pwyll, lost somewhere in the desert, the sand and stone hidden by ice and snow. Now, that comforting lie had been shattered by the truth.

He was in Cocytus, a frozen corner of Hell.

He was struck by the profound realization that Pwyll and Seven Rivers; which, also meant his father's kingdom, and with it, his home, were all impossibly far away. He looked to Eideothea. 'I'm completely dependent on her.' He thought. 'She holds my life in her hands. A dark elf. My enemy.' He looked to the gelugon. 'A devil worshipper.'

The dialogue of clicks between Eideothea and the gelugon became furious. Lewin could tell from Eideothea's body language that the two were engaged in an argument. The thought of it filled him with fear. He assumed that the gelugon, small or not, could easily kill them. He could not fathom why she would argue with such a creature.

The beating of his heart began to quicken. He felt the need to take some self-preserving action. He had the fear-inspired thought of scrambling back down the ice, to the bottom of the crevasse, where the gelugon could not fit. He then remembered that his crampons and the climbing pick had been packed away. He looked from Eideothea to the gelugon. He knew there was nothing he could do.

Eideothea waved her arm in a signal of defeat. She turned. Lewin saw that her mouth was twisted in disgust. The gelugon rose erect, turned, and began to slowly and awkwardly walk forward.

"Greedy." Eideothea muttered to herself.

"I'm glad it didn't kill us," admitted Lewin.

Eideothea lifted her goggles and looked at him with her blood-soaked eyes. "I doubt he would get away with it." She turned her head and looked at the retreating gelugon. "He saw an opportunity to threaten, that's all." She looked back to Lewin. "I promised him a future boon. I paid him off, in effect, to convince him to carry on with his duties."

Lewin didn't know what to say. He looked from Eideothea to the gelugon. The dialogue, even though he had witnessed it, was impossible to comprehend.

"He leads, we follow," said Eideothea, as she picked up the pack.

. . .

Although the gelugon's legs were much longer, his manner of walking was laborious and slow. It was easy to keep up with him. Lewin scanned the plateau. It was ringed with mountains of snow-capped black stone. One of the mountains, far to Lewin's left, emitted a column of black smoke. The wind carried the smoke high above the mountains, spreading it over the peaks like a think blanket of black wool.

43

Lewin had to squint his eyes to block out the light. He followed the jagged line of the peaks that separated sky from ground. He paused, realizing there was something above the peak directly in front of them, something obscured by the volcano's sky-borne ash. All he could discern was its rough diamond shape and its deep black color.

A wind picked up, racing down from the mountain. Both he and Eideothea gathered closer behind the gelugon. His massive body partially shielded them. Lewin bowed his head, allowing the fur of his hood to bear the brunt of the wind. He lifted his hand and covered his lower face with his glove.

He marched without thinking. It was too cold for the working of the mind. Several times he thoughtlessly veered from behind the gelugon. A blast of cold wind greeted him, advising him to correct course. After a seemingly endless march the gelugon stopped. Prince Lewin lifted his head and looked around.

Foothills of black stone reached up from the snow and ice. Before these rose a narrow field of wind-carved ice crags. The image of the flaying gloves, their metal shards glinting in the candlelight, sprang from Lewin's memory, sending a shiver down his spine. He realized that both Eideothea and the gelugon were staring at him. He looked self-consciously from one to the other.

The gelugon turned and looked up. He extended his leg and unfurled his pincer, pointing. Prince Lewin followed the motion. He could better make out the object hovering above the peaks. It appeared to be an enormous piece of rock, large enough to support a city, held aloft by some unknown force. A collection of ice-encrusted chains dropped from the bottom of the stone and disappeared behind the peaks. 'If I can see them at this distance,' thought Lewin, 'they must be truly massive.' The gelugon's clicking returned Lewin's attention to the creature.

"The Lofty House," translated Eideothea. Lewin looked to her, then back up to the chain-held rock.

"He will take us no further," said Eideothea. "You must lead us from here."

"Me?" asked Lewin.

The gelugon leapt into the air. A pair of wings opened, raining snow down on Eideothea and Lewin. The gelugon buzzed overhead, riding the outgoing winds. With the creature no longer providing cover, the wind bit into Lewin's exposed skin. He turned his back to it. "How should I know where to go?" he yelled over the howling of the wind.

"There's a cave ahead," advised Eideothea.

"So, lead us there."

"A path cuts through the crags. You must lead the way."

The wind blew down her hood. Her hair wiped about her face. She seemed unconcerned. Lewin frowned. He preferred the shelter of a cave to the exposure of the open air. 'If she wants me to lead, so be it,' he thought. He turned and began towards the opening in the ribbon of ice.

The crags lifted the wind above them, allowing for a relative calm. Lewin kept his eyes on the path. He realized that Eideothea was falling behind. He turned to her. She was standing some distance behind him, her fly-eyed goggles in her hand, looking at him. He waved her forward. She did not move or acknowledge his gesture.

'What's wrong with her?' he wondered. He heard a dull thud to his right. He realized the sound had been at the edge of his awareness since he began to walk among the crags. He looked from Eideothea to the ice crag beside him. It was perhaps twice as tall as him, thicker at the base then at the tip, like a stalagmite of ice rising from the white floor.

At first he saw nothing except the shimmering surface of blue-white. The thudding grew louder. He glanced at Eideothea. Her expression was unchanged. He returned his attention to the crag. A shadow seemed to pass over and through the ice. He stepped closer. He saw a man. It was the soldier who had been trapped under the ice outside of Pwyll. He ran the rest of the distance. He lifted his fur-gloved hands and placed them against the ice.

'Yes, it's him!' Lewin thought.

"I'll get you out." He turned to Eideothea. "Come here!" he yelled. He pointed to the pack. "I need the ice pick! Hurry." He turned back to the trapped soldier. As before, the soldier was banging his fist against the ice. "I'll break you out!" yelled Lewin. He turned and stepped towards Eideothea. "Hurry!"

She did not move. Lewin looked to the trapped soldier and motioned that the man should remain patient. The pained pleading in the man's eyes troubled him. Lewin ran down the path to Eideothea.

"I need the pack," he said, reaching for the bag. Eideothea dropped her shoulder back, moving the strap of the bag out of Lewin's reach. She eyed him, the feature of her face hard, her blood-soaked eyes merciless. This gave him pause. Eideothea looked from him to the closest crag of ice. Lewin followed her gaze.

'Another soldier!' He turned and looked at a third spike of ice. It too acted as a prison. He spun and stepped to yet another crag. He lifted his hand and wiped the snow from the folds of ice. A man's face, his eyes filled with panic, looked out from the ice. Lewin stumbled backwards. "My father's men," he gasped. He turned to Eideothea. "You knew."

She looked from the crag to him.

"That's why you wanted me to lead the way. To shock me."

"To educate you."

"How many?" he asked, his voice trembling.

"As many as I could get beneath the ice."

"Why?"

"To honor Baalzebul."

Lewin advanced towards Eideothea, intent on the pack and the picks within. He grabbed the pack.

"You can't free them—that way."

She willingly let the pack pass from her to him. He reached into it and pulled free an ice pick. He walked back to the ice crag that imprisoned the soldier he had now seen twice. He lifted the pick and brought it down against the ice. With a sharp crack the tip of the pick broke, spun high into the air, arcing over and behind him, and disappeared amongst the crags. He turned to Eideothea.

"How?" He rushed her, grabbed her by the front of her fur coat, and pulled her close.

"—kill you," he hissed.

"Their fates have not yet been decided."

"They're locked in unbreakable ice." He jerked her body. "You said—"

"I owe an offering," she stated. "The souls of your father's men would please my master."

"Souls," echoed Lewin. He glanced to the ice crag to his right. The man within stood morose, his eyes vacant.

"Unless I can offer him something—else."

Lewin looked back to her. "Me?"

He pushed her away, waving the broken ice pick between them. "That's blackmail," he countered. "You said an oath given under duress—"

Eideothea stepped towards him. Her features softened. "All I ask is that you grant him an honest audience. Listen to him. Hear his words with an open mind."

"If I refuse? You'll give him—"

"I ask so little," said Eideothea. "I ask you only to listen." She paused, giving Lewin a space to speak. He remained silent. "If only you'll hear him out, perhaps," she looked to the crags.

"You're evil," stated Prince Lewin. "You condemn these honest men."

"Do I?" She stepped closer to Lewin. "How did these men come to me? Who sent them? Who condemned them?"

Lewin looked into her blood-soaked eyes. "They were brave men, loyal men."

"They were tools. Your father knows that. Your father sent these men to face a foe he knew was capable of —" She let her words go unspoken.

"You accuse my father—"

"Of being a king," interjected Eideothea. "Of being a ruler."

"Of being evil! He isn't! He's not like you!"

"No, Prince Lewin," countered Eideothea, her tone gentle. "He didn't send those men to fight a demonic foe because he was foolish or callous, but because he was wise."

Lewin looked at her.

"To lead means to accept a terrible responsibility." She stepped up to Lewin and placed her hands on his shoulders. "Your father sent you so you could lead, to show you, the terrible blade that hangs over the throne. It is not a comfortable chair to occupy."

"My father—"

"He can't help you," interjected Eideothea. "He can't help these men now. He can't save their souls." Lewin looked down into her blood-washed eyes. "*You* can, Lewin. You can lead. Baalzebul led the army of fallen angels as they stormed Heaven's gate. It was Baalzebul's wisdom that freed the multitudes from the yoke of their oppressor. He can teach you. He can fill you with the wisdom of his experience."

"A devil?" whispered prince Lewin. "A—fallen angel."

The fear and helplessness captured in Lewin's contorted features, held in the freezing tears welling up in his eyes, caused Eideothea to hold her counter-argument. She pressed cheek against his chest.

"Share my warmth, let me share yours." She looked up at him. She identified his vulnerability. She grabbed his hand in hers and led him to the cave. He followed her without looking up. He couldn't bring himself to meet the gazes of the trapped men.

. . .

Lewin was thankful for her warmth. He lay with her, skin-to-skin, in the furs. The flies crawled from her to him, as before, but he hardly noticed their activity. He could not see her. He knew her only by touch. By the curves of her feminine form pressing down on him.

He traced his fingers along her back. He defined the shape of her muscle with his touch. His fingers ran over something rough. A scabbed-over cut. He gingerly explored the cut. It was little more than a scratch, really, and seemed harmless. As he touched her wound he realized she was kissing his chest.

He remembered her question, 'Are you a virgin?' He lifted his other hand and placed it on the small of her back. He felt the twin dimples on either side of her spine. The bottom of his palm felt the rise of her muscles, as they lifted and formed the curve of her butt. She partially lifted and he felt her erect nipples brush against him. She wiggled her body up his. He knew she was searching for his lips with her own.

He turned his head to the side. He dropped his hands from her body. "Why do you torment me?"

"Most men consider this pleasure, not torment."

"You are a dark elf witch. A devil worshipper. You've trapped men's souls. Now you tempt me."

She paused. He could feel her smile. "You were willing enough to lie with me."

"Survival."

"Just survival?" She reached down and picked up his hand. He did not pull away. She guided his hand onto her butt. She moved his hand over her. After allowing it for a moment, Lewin jerked his hand away. Eideothea sighed. She rest her head on his chest. She could hear the pounding of his heart. She could feel the conflict in him. "How old is your father?"

Lewin did not answer.

"You are his only son, his heir."

"Am I?"

"Lewin," She lifted her head to look at his face, although he could not see hers. "We have spies in your father's court." He turned his head to face her. "I know you are his heir. He sent you to Pwyll because he expected victory. He wanted you to return to the capital on the wings of glory." She set her cheek against the muscles of his chest.

"I failed him," whispered Lewin. "I failed those men out there." He lifted his arms and wrapped them around Eideothea's thin waist. He clutched her close, finding comfort in her presence, despite everything he knew about her.

"Your father miscalculated," she said. "He underestimated us."

"When kings error—"

"Men die," finished Eideothea. "His defeat will shake the people's confidence in him," continued Eideothea. "The people worry about you. My people gloat. They were quick to communicate that they held you prisoner—for a time." She could feel Lewin's eyes on her. "The stability of your father's rule is in doubt. The heir is gone. People hate uncertainty more than anything else."

"I'm not dead. I'm not gone. I'm captured." Despite knowing he should feel anger and resentment, he didn't. He traced his fingers along Eideothea's hips, crossed his arms, lifted them, and touched the jutting blades of her shoulders. "An honest audience?"

"That's all he asks of you," said Eideothea.

"And the men?" He struggled over his words, "their souls."

"Their fates have not yet been decided."

"Until I decide," concluded Prince Lewin. "And if I reject him? Is that the horrible fate you spoke of?"

Eideothea did not answer. Instead, she resumed her gentle kissing. Lewin did not protest. The brush of her lips electrified his skin. He felt a wave of energy work its way through his flesh, sending his blood to the surface as goose-pimples. He shuddered. Eideothea sprang forward. Her face hovered just above his. He could feel her breath on his face. He could feel the moisture of her mouth close to his.

He feared her kiss but he didn't turn away from it. Eideothea leaned closer. He lifted his head. The edge of their lips touched. Eideothea pulled back. She extended her tongue and licked his lips. "Have you been saving yourself for a princess?"

He tried to kiss her but she pulled back further. This confused him. He felt unsure of himself, of her. He set his head back against the furs. She leaned forward and touched her lips to his once more. She drug her lips over his, spreading her moisture to him.

"An arranged marriage," he answered. "A wife, to produce an heir."

"A queen?" She took his top lip between her teeth and bit down, not hard enough to draw blood, but enough to cause pain. Lewin turned his head, freeing his lip. He immediately turned his head back.

'I'll be king.' The thought never felt so real as it did now. He wondered, 'will I? Will I ever escape this frozen Hell?' He pictured the soldier under the ice, then saw him again, *in* the ice. Scattered thoughts coalesced in his mind. Eideothea was nibbling at his neck. He grabbed her shoulders. Her face hovered over his, although he could not see it. "Is that the horrible fate you can save me from? To rule—unwisely?"

She did not answer. In the silence his thoughts went to her nude body. To the sensation of her on him. He felt the softness of her skin. It was contrasted by the roughness of her scabs. He realized he had completely forgotten about, and could not even feel, the activity of the flies. He wondered if they were still present. This thought was overrun by a growing sensation.

He could feel her heart beating close to his. It seemed as if their two hearts beat in one body. He knew the location of her mouth. He lifted his head and parted her lips with his own. She twisted her head, forming a loose seal with their lips, and lowered her agile tongue into his mouth. His tongue rose to greet hers.

"You can return to your life," she whispered. She kissed him, passionately, then lifted her head. "You can be prince once more. The people will rejoice at your return."

He returned her kiss. She pulled away. "You can be king. You *will* be king. He can guide you."

"Baalzebul?"

"The Lord of Flies," breathed Eideothea. "The White Son."

"A devil," countered Lewin. He pushed against her, holding her shoulders off of him. "A dark elf witch," he accused her, but his voice held no resolve in it.

"Lewin," whispered Eideothea. "*You* are the White Son. You are the Prince of—" She reached down, sliding her fingers down his abdomen. "Lewin," she whispered. She pressed her body against his. "*My* prince," she breathed. "*My* king."

Lewin pulled her to him. He took her lips in his. She kissed him then lifted her head. She locked eyes with him.

"Take me my king. Conquer me."

. . .

Lewin lay on his side, drifting at the edge of sleep. He held Eideothea's smaller frame in his arms. "Why do you hurt yourself?"

"To honor him," she said, her voice reverent.

"He requires it?"

"What is pleasure without pain?" she asked. "What is loyalty without sacrifice?" She turned her head and brought her hand to his cheek. "Even a king must pay a price. The greatest price of all."

"To suffer for his people?"

"If you wish to lead them, yes. To lead a people is to suffer for them."

The souls trapped in ice came to his mind. "To send men to their deaths."

"To have the resolve to do so, to demand that sacrifice. Only Baalzebul can teach you such strength." She lowered her hand and turned, snuggling closer to him.

"Baalzebul," whispered prince Lewin.

"A great general, a wise leader."

"A fallen angel?"

"A righteous rebel."

"He knew what must be done?"

"He knew," said Eideothea. "He had the courage of his convictions."

"I can't imagine doing as my father did, sending an army against such a treacherous foe."

Eideothea turned her head and looked at him out of the corners of her eyes. "All foes are treacherous." She turned further and kissed him, before turning back.

"I was taught war," said Lewin, speaking almost to himself as much as to her. "I read treaties on battle, spoke to experienced soldiers. I learned about the machinations of court intrigue." Eideothea spun to face him. They looked into each other's eyes. Lewin continued. "I've been schooled on every aspect of rule," he chuckled. "But somehow, I wasn't ready. I—"

"It's all abstract," said Eideothea, reaching up to caress his face, "the reality is—"

"Men died because I failed to—"

"Not you."

"Yes, me. I was in charge," said prince Lewin. "I'm the—"

"General Ord wouldn't have listened to you, even if you had commanded him to do differently than he did. We knew that." She smiled. "Don't forget, we had spies. We knew his character intimately."

"Did you know mine?"

"I do now," said Eideothea.

"No, that's not what I mean," said Lewin. "Did you —plan," he studied her face. "All this?"

"Did I plan on risking my life to snatch you away from bickering demons?" She laughed. "No, my king, that was stupidly impulsive of me." She kissed him then pulled back and looked into his eyes. "No, when I saw you drug in and tossed at their feet, when I looked upon this face," she touched his lips with her fingertips, "I saw the great soul within. It shone even through closed eyes." Lewin had never been spoken to in such a way. He felt a mixture of embarrassment and pride swell up in him. Eideothea was studying him. "I knew you would achieve greatness, if only you received the right—insights."

"Baalzebul?"

"Yes, only he—"

"Can teach me the final lesson," finished Prince Lewin. "The wisdom all my wise instructors couldn't impart?" Eideothea didn't speak, she gazed into his eyes. "But—a devil. How can I—"

"Condemned, yes," said Eideothea. "But by whom? By a just creator? Ask yourself, if there was no injustice, why would there be those willing to risk eternal damnation to rise up?" Lewin had no answer. "I cannot force you to accept my master," said Eideothea. "I can only beg you, for your own sake, to listen to him, to accept his teachings."

Lewin nodded, saying yes with his eyes.

"You—"

"I am prepared to—to accept his wisdom."

Eideothea kissed him. She rolled over and pulled his arms around her. "You're youthful vigor wore me out." She curled into him. Lewin held her in his arms. He rested his head against the furs and closed his eyes. His breathing followed hers. The beating of his heart matched the rhythm of hers.

. . .

"Prince Lewin." The voice was distant, as if whispered from across the room. He stirred but did not open his eyes. "Prince Lewin. Wake up."

Lewin opened his eyes. He realized at once that he was in the cell. The hard, cold, stone floor had replaced the comfort of the furs. There remained, however, a lingering warmth in his arms. 'Eideothea.' He remembered holding her as they fell asleep. He remembered making love to her. He felt for her. Only the stone greeted his hands.

"Eideothea?"

No light came from the slot in the door. He crawled on his hands and knees, searching. His palms found something rich in texture, warm and wet. He could not see the blood on his hands, but he knew it from the smell and touch of it. The blood formed a trail that led to the door.

"Eideothea?" He wiped the blood on his pants and felt around the cell. It was empty. When he reached the door he realized it was not shut tightly, as it had been. The trail of blood led under the door. He edged his fingers into the gap and pulled the door open. The hall was as dark as the cell. He crawled through the door way. His palms and knees slipped in the fresh blood.

"Eideothea?" he called, a bit louder. He heard the striking of a match. A flame leapt from the darkness. He blinked his eyes. The flame went to a candle. He could not tell who had lit the candle. He did, however, hear the person's footsteps as they moved away from him. It was not the sound of hard soles on stone, but of bare feet.

"Eideothea?" His voice echoed back to him. He rose and approached the candle. His bare feet picked up the blood, despite his efforts to avoid it. The candle was in a brass holder, sitting on the floor. He could see the splatter of blood around it. He tried to look down the hall, but saw nothing. He bent and picked up the candle holder. His blood-smeared hand came into view.

'Is this real?' He asked himself. He could feel the feeble heat from the flame, the cold of the stone beneath his feet. He felt the pain of hunger. He felt the ache of fatigue in his muscles and bones. He had never felt such pain and discomfort in a dream. 'More magic?' he asked himself. 'More lies?'

He caught the fragrance of Eideothea on him. The smell of her sex emanated from his body, from his groin, from his fingers, from his lips. These carnal odors mixed with the smell of blood. The mixture clouded his thinking. He shook his head, trying to free his mind from the fog.

He advanced down the hall. It was straight, carved, not natural. The trail of splattered blood continued. The light from his candle crept onto a wooden door. He stared at it in shock. 'I know this door,' he thought. 'My father's crest.' He held the candle closer. He reached out and touched the embossed surface. When he pulled his fingers back the royal crest was streaked with blood.

He looked at the door pull. He reached to it, lifted it, releasing the latch, and pushed the door away from him. Light greeted him. Not sunlight, for the windows in the room were hidden behind thick curtains. The room was illuminated with the light from candles and from the fire in the hearth. He stepped into the room. 'My father's bedroom.' He thought. 'No, not quite.' He realized that there were subtle differences. Things had been moved, a tapestry, a table, an added sitting chair, making two where before there had been one. Other things had been added. A wardrobe, doors open, a woman's dresses spilling out.

He set the candle down on a table. He walked to a window and pulled the curtain back. There was no window pane. In its place was a wall of ice. The life-draining cold reached out to him. He closed the curtain.

"Lewin."

He spun. He saw her for a moment as she stood behind the room's second door. She moved, disappearing from view. "Eideothea!" He ran to the door, flung it fully open, and looked for her. She was gone. What he saw instead was the throne room. 'My father's throne room.'

He passed the threshold and stood, looking. Once again, like the bedroom behind him, there were subtle changes. As if a new occupant had brought their own personal taste to bear. "Eideothea?" He walked into the room. He felt the warmth and slickness of blood. He looked down and saw that the trail continued. His eyes searched the room. "Don't hide from me." He commanded. "You've no need for magic after what we've shared. Dispel this illusion."

He followed the blood, convinced that it was hers. It went to the throne. He stopped and looked down. Sitting on the cushion was a single fly. Its wing lying flat. A leg lifted high, bent, and scrapped the surface of the wing, cleaning it. He reached down, intent on swiping at the fly. An ebony hand grabbed his wrist. He looked.

She smiled at him. He noticed that her skin was unblemished. Her hair was carefully combed and done in plaits. She wore a form-fitting dress, cut low in the front, revealing the curves of her breasts. No flies crawled on her skin. He turned to face her. He looked into her blood-washed eyes.

"This isn't—"

She lifted a finger to his lips. "Shhh," she smiled. "Sit, my king." She looked to the throne. The fly took flight, buzzing between them. Eideothea rested her hands on Lewin's shoulders. She pushed him gently to the throne. Then she climbed into his lap. She leaned into him and began to kiss and bite at the soft skin of his neck. Lewin felt himself weaken at her touch. He wrapped one hand around her, resting the other on the arms of the throne.

Something tickled the ring finger of his free hand. He lifted his hand to view, resting it on the curve of Eideothea's hip. The fly had landed on his finger. It sat there, facing him. 'Where the royal signet ring—' Lewin did not finish his thought. He had the desire to wave his hand, to shake the fly free, but, just as the thought entered his mind, a flash of pain came from his abdomen, where either the guard or Eideothea had jabbed him. He didn't know which was real. The sensation traveled through his body, shuddering him. Just as the pain died down Eideothea took the lobe of his ear between her lips. She began to suck on it. The pleasure, such a contrast to the pain, made Lewin's head swim.

He stared into the fly's compound eyes. His attention turned inwards, to the sensations his body felt, the pleasure from Eideothea's gentle kisses and playful biting. She ran her long, delicate fingers through his hair. Her other hand cupped his neck, pulling him closer to her. "My king," she whispered. "The King of Flies."

Lewin's attention went back to the fly. It was motionless, regarding him with an intensity far beyond the powers of a mere insect. His own multifaceted reflection sunk him into a trance. He blinked. He was staring into Eideothea's fly-eyed mask.

He blinked again and looked at her in totality. She was sitting cross-legged in front of him. He too was sitting cross-legged. The throne room was no more. They sat in the cave in which they had made love. Above them, far above them, above the mountain peak, floated the Lofty House.

Eideothea held her arms out. They were covered with fresh blood and flies. Eideothea was holding something in her hands. Lewin realized she was holding his hands in hers. His arms, too, were extended. His arms, too, were covered in fresh blood and flies. She was chanting, as before, only, unlike before, now he could understand her.

"—took Moloch and Nybbas into his confidence and showed them the way to victory." She was saying. Lewin looked down. He was bare-chested. His torso was covered in blood. "When it came time for the Exodus from Heaven," continued Eideothea, "to break the chains of light, the oppression of the Creator, who lifted the fiery sword? Who struck the first blow? Baalzebul! The White Son!"

The stone of the cave walls flew apart without sound. For a second, blinding white light filled his eyes. It was the light of the ice-coated plain. When his vision returned the light was gone. In its place rose the steep, ice-carved walls of the Lofty House. Eideothea hovered in the foreground, a shimmering, indistinct presence. A second presence came into focus.

He was a perfectly formed being, an angel. He sat, bare chested, his skin as white and pristine as newly fallen snow. His waist was wrapped in white cloth trimmed in gold. He sat on a throne made of ice. His white-blonde hair cascaded over the flawless musculature of his shoulders. He studied Lewin with ice-blue eyes—a blue extended to an infinite depth.

'Baalzebul,' thought Lewin. The presence radiated such inhuman beauty that he was difficult to accept as real. Yet, his eyes, 'his eyes,' thought Lewin. 'So cruel. Completely without compassion.' Just like ice.

Baalzebul leaned forward. His wings unfolded behind him. They were not wings of white feathers. They were without distinct form, merely the suggestion of form, dark, shifting, buzzing. Lewin realized that Baalzebul's wings were composed of thousands, 'No,' he thought, 'hundreds of thousands,' of flies.

The twin clouds of flies changed their shape. They no longer loosely resembled two wings, but became tendrils. With an almost imperceptible nod of Baalzebul's head the tendrils of flies curled. Their tips turned towards Lewin. With a horrifying cacophony of buzzing the tendrils shot out. The flies reached for Lewin. He cringed. They moved past him. He turned to follow their movement. The tips of the fly-composed tendrils moved over a body suspended behind Lewin. The merciless biting of the flies caused the man to scream.

He seemed half alive. He was nude. His head hung so that his dirty, blood-clotted hair—once the same color as Lewin's—hid his face. His skin was a tapestry of pain; cuts, bruises, lacerations, welts, flaps of skin hung from his torso. Flies burrowed into his tissue, biting as deep as bone.

"What of those who defy the White Son?" asked Eideothea. "What of those who reject the loving hand of the master?" Her voice was intimate, in contrast to the angry buzzing of the flies and pained screaming of the tortured man. "Do they not hang—bloody, torn, defeated, filled with regret for their treachery—in the Lofty House? Let the foes of Baalzebul think of the tortures that await them should they act against the Lord of Flies. Let those who prove their loyalty to the White Son feed on the betrayer's blood. Let them get fat on his sorrow."

Lewin looked from the half-dead man to the Lord of Flies. A malice-filled smile spread across his perfectly sculpted face. His ice-blue eyes flashed with a sinister light.

"You have accepted him," said Eideothea. "He has accepted you." She squeezed his hands. "You will be king. I will be your queen. I am with child, my King." Lewin's gaze shot from the fallen angel to the dark elf woman gripping his hands. She smiled. The act did not fill him with comfort. "I carry your heir within me." Lewin was so stunned he could not speak. Eideothea continued. "You will rule a nation. You will command a people." Her gaze shifted to Baalzebul. "But he will be master."

A pained cry turned Lewin's attention to the shackled, tortured presence. The man screamed and threw his head back. Lewin looked into the agony-twisted face.

It was his own.

H. Rad Bethlen has been compared to Isak Dinesen (*Seven Gothic Tales*) and Fritz Leiber (*Swords and Deviltry*). He is known for his work in the fantasy and horror genres as well as his non-fiction. He has been published in Europe and America.

Enjoy the story?

If you liked what you read, please take a moment to **leave a review on Amazon**! Your feedback helps other readers find this story. It only takes a minute but it makes a huge difference. The Amazon algorithm requires 30-50 reviews before it will pick this book up and promote it to like-minded readers. Your review is instrumental in helping that happen!

For more great fiction and non-fiction please visit:

roosterandravenpublishing.com

hradbethlen.com

or H. Rad Bethlen's Amazon page.